*For my boys, Chase and Griffin Murphy—who are now young men, kind and impactful.
And all the boys I've taught and the young men I've coached from Ronnie Garrison to
Andrew Note to Markus Stevenson to the lasting memory of #89, Shamus Digney . . .*
— Frank

For my brother, the world could use more boys like you.
— Kayla

Thank you to the little village of pre-readers who helped this book along. Carla,
Haley, my dad, and my family, for your support, including Jumper, for sitting next to
me for countless hours as I wrote and revised! Some of my teaching family—Colin
McCarthy, Ro Carcaci-Foster, Christine Bailey, Amy Smith, Allie Bailey, the Caraccios,
the Mingaccis, the Wetherills, Kiley Malloy (my favorite poet), and especially Barbara
Dan and her family. In my KidLit family: Olivia Van Ledtje, you are an epic force of nature.
Paige Britt, you are pure goodness! Tami Charles, for your guidance. And Kathy
Morrison, my independent bookseller! Sarah Rockett—for being the champion of
and collaborator in creating this book; you are a phenomenal editor! Kayla Harren,
for illuminating this text beyond my imagining, and the team at Sleeping Bear Press.
Heather Hughes, for believing in me again, almost twenty years later—many thanks!
— Frank

Sleeping Bear Press™

2395 South Huron Parkway, Suite 200, Ann Arbor, MI 48104
www.sleepingbearpress.com
© Sleeping Bear Press
Printed and bound in the United States.
10 9 8 7 6 5 4 3 2

Library of Congress Cataloging-in-Publication Data
Names: Murphy, Frank, 1966- author. | Harren, Kayla, illustrator.
Title: A boy like you / by Frank Murphy ; illustrated by Kayla Harren.
Description: Ann Arbor, MI : Sleeping Bear Press, [2019] | Summary:
Encourages every boy to embrace all of the things that make him
unique, and to be curious, brave, kind, thoughtful, and more.
Identifiers: LCCN 2019010249 | ISBN 9781534110465 (hardcover)
Subjects: | CYAC: Conduct of life--Fiction. | Individuality--Fiction.
Classification: LCC PZ7.1.M8724 Boy 2019 | DDC [E]--dc23
LC record available at https://lccn.loc.gov/2019010249

A BOY like YOU

By Frank Murphy and Illustrated by Kayla Harren

PUBLISHED BY SLEEPING BEAR PRESS

There are billions and
billions
and **billions**
of people in the world.

But you are the only YOU there is!

And the world needs a boy like you.

The world needs a boy . . .

to be kind and helpful.

To be smart and strong.

Maybe your "strong" is making sure everyone has a chance to play.

Maybe your "smart" is knowing the precisely right, perfect pass to make.

Oh boy, be you.

The YOU that makes you feel most alive.

Play hard, but play fair.
Be a great teammate.

Say "Nice goal!" and "Good try!"
Don't say "You throw like a girl." *Ever.*

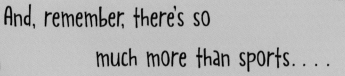

And, remember, there's so
much more than sports. . . .

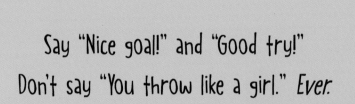

There are vegetable gardens to grow.
And flowers to give.

There are cakes to bake.
(And eat, too!)

There are instruments to
play and songs to sing.

There are stories to read
and stories to write.

There are science experiments to do.
And math problems to solve.

Oh boy, be curious.

Take a risk and raise your hand.
Smart kids ask questions.
So ask a lot of them!
The more you know—the less you'll fear.

Here's a secret that not many people know.
Fear and bravery are partners.
You can't be brave without first being afraid.

If you're not ready to be brave—
ask for help. This shows you're smart.

Sometimes, you may feel like crying.
Cry. This shows you're strong.
One day you'll be a man, and men cry too.

Oh boy, dream big.

You are unique—and your dreams are yours to dream.

It's okay to not know exactly what you want to be—or what you will become.

But whatever you become—become a good one.

And remember this about dreams:
You don't get what you wish for; you get what you work for.
So work hard for what you want.

In this world, you will meet all kinds of people—
and all of them are different.

Ask people to tell you their stories.
Then listen. Listen hard.
Stories connect all of us.
They're part of what makes us who we are.
Don't forget to tell your own story too.

As you travel, and come and go,
 hug your family and high-five your friends.
  High-five your family and hug your friends.

Walk with your head up—
you'll want to see where you're going.

Smile at people and say hello.

Leave every place you visit . . . better than you found it.

And leave every person . . .
better than you found them.

Say "Please."
Say "Thank you."
Say "I love you."
(And if that's not exactly right,
simply say "I like you.")

And, maybe most importantly, say
"How may I help?"

Helping each other is the best way
to make our world stronger.

Oh boy, be thoughtful.

Eat lunch with the new kid.

Hold the door for the
person behind you.

Do the right thing, even
when no one is looking.

And most of all . . . be you.
You'll discover that the best you
is the you that is ALL you. . . .

Not a little you and a little someOne else.
You are original. And that's a wonderful thing.

And always remember,
the world needs a boy . . .
a smart boy,
a brave boy,
a kind boy.

Oh boy,
a boy like YOU!

Author's Note *about* Being Strong

Sometimes boys grow up believing that the best way to be a boy is to be a strong boy—physically tough and emotionally hard. They believe the most important things are how good they are at sports or how strong their muscles are—and that boys who don't fit into that mold are less important. Remember, there are many ways to be strong and all those ways are what makes us unique. Being strong isn't just about muscles. Muscles are part of being strong on the "outside." There's "inside" strength too.

The strength inside you guides the things that you do and say. How many examples of "inside" strength can you find in this book? (Hint: there are a lot!) And remember—there are many more things to learn about being a boy and about being you! Keep learning! What strengths make you unique? The world needs a boy just like you, the one and only YOU!

From *the* Author

Through teaching elementary school for the larger part of three decades, coaching baseball and basketball, and being a parent of boys, I see boys growing up in a world that sends them confusing messages about many things. One of those things is masculinity. Many messages about masculinity can be toxic—dangerous to the development of young minds and hearts of boys, and to those around them. I've watched too many boys go out to recess (where sports dominate) feeling undervalued because sports are not their passion. I've watched boys be steered away from some of the arts—like crafts, theater, and singing—by the adults in their lives. We've all watched male leaders be rewarded for swagger and bluster and greed. This must change. Each generation's best future rests with its children. These children can become leaders who honor humanity—leaders with open hearts and minds who accept the uniqueness of individuals, regardless of their differences.

The messages in this book teach leadership skills that I believe help all young people gain real strength. They teach kindness (which is a high-level leadership skill!) and compassion. And I hope the messages in this book help boys and men (young and old—it's never too late) to better understand their own lives, to develop their unique voices and talents so they can thrive, and to help make the world a better place. The world needs a boy—a strong and brave and kind boy—now more than ever.

— Frank Murphy